Lunch Bunnies

by Kathryn Lasky

Illustrated by

Marylin Hafner

To Molly,
HAVE A nice
Lunch!

Kathryn Lasky
1996

Little, Brown and Company
Boston New York Toronto London

First Edition

Library of Congress Cataloging-in-Publication Data

Lasky, Kathryn.
    Lunch bunnies / by Kathryn Lasky ; illustrated by Marylin Hafner.
— 1st ed.
        p.   cm.
    Summary: Clyde the rabbit is ready to start school, but after talking with
his brother, he is worried about what will happen at lunchtime.
    ISBN 0-316-51525-6
    [1. Schools — Fiction. 2. Rabbits — Fiction.] I. Hafner, Marylin,
ill. II. Title.
PZ7.L3274Lu   1996
[E] — dc20   92-31554

                    10 9 8 7 6 5 4 3 2 1

                            NIL

            Published simultaneously in Canada by
            Little, Brown & Company (Canada) Limited
            and in Great Britain by Little, Brown
                and Company (UK) Limited

                    Printed in Italy

For Max and Meribah,
once-upon-a-time lunch bunnies
— K. L.

For Zoë, Katherine S., and Sarah
— M. H.

Clyde was practicing. He was carrying a tray with a small carton of milk, an orange, and a peanut butter and jelly sandwich across the kitchen to the table. The orange began a slow roll toward the milk carton. Clyde stopped walking and tipped the tray slightly to make it level.

"That's great!" said his mom, watching him.

Tomorrow was Clyde's first day of school. He was ready to learn how to read and ready to learn how to write, but he was not ready for lunch.

"You better hope they don't have soup," his older brother, Jefferson, muttered.

"They won't have soup on the first day of school," said their mother. "That would be too much for first graders like Clyde."

"You never know!" Jefferson said.

"Oh!" gasped Clyde. He could just hear a big wet *splat* of soup on the cafeteria floor.

"Yeah," said Jefferson as if he were reading Clyde's thoughts. "If the soup spills, the lunch ladies make you clean it up! And you *really* better hope they don't have mystery goosh."

"What's mystery goosh?" asked Clyde, trying to keep his voice as steady as the tray.

"Well," said Jefferson, "you know how you hate food that touches, like when the applesauce slops into the green beans and the beet juice runs into the mashed potatoes and makes them pink?"

"Yeah...," said Clyde slowly.

"That's what mystery goosh is," said Jefferson. "Except at school, the cooks do it on purpose. They goosh up all these foods together — peas, carrots, a little yogurt — some cottage cheese for good measure. And you have to eat every bite."

SUPERB!

"Jefferson!" their mother said sharply. "Don't go making up nonsense and frightening your brother."

"It's not nonsense, Mom, and mystery goosh *is* frightening. It's yuck."

Mystery goosh — Clyde hadn't heard about that, but he had heard about the lunch ladies — Gloria and old Mrs. Twig and Frances. They were very large and very bristly. They had scratchy voices and yelled at anyone who didn't finish his lunch or was too noisy.

Lunch was beginning to sound horrible.

When Clyde went to bed, he said to his mother, "We should have practiced with soup."

"Don't worry. You'll do just fine," his mom said.

"But what if…" Clyde swallowed hard.

"What if what?" his mom asked.

"What if no one wants to eat lunch with me?" he whispered.

"Don't be silly, Clyde. You'll make friends. I like eating lunch with you."

"But you're my mother. That doesn't count."

"Well, even if I weren't, I'd still want to eat lunch with you." Clyde tried to imagine her short and eating lunch in a school cafeteria. It was hard.

That night, Clyde dreamed about cafeteria lines miles long where you had to carry your tray up hills and over mountains, across rivers and down through valleys. There were scolding lunch ladies around every bend making you mop up spilled soup. And there was no one to help him. He felt so alone.

The next morning, Clyde's mother put his lunch money into a special little envelope. She made sure to give him the exact amount so he wouldn't have to get change.

"Now, what are you going to do when you get in the lunch line, Clyde?" she asked.

"I get the tray from the stack. I put it on the counter to slide it along. I get out my envelope and open it up so the money lady can get it easy."

"You won't have time to do all that," Jefferson interrupted. "Everybody's in a hurry. They're not going to want to wait around while old Clyde takes out his envelope, drops a dime or two on the floor…"

"Hush, Jefferson!" said their mother sharply. She turned to Clyde. "You're going to do just fine, dear." And she kissed them both good-bye.

All morning long, Clyde worried. He worried through Circle Time, through reading, and through art, though he did learn how to read his first word and made a nice picture.

Then the teacher announced, "Lunchtime! Please have your lunch money ready. And remember, no shoving in line."

Shoving! Clyde hadn't heard about this. The thought was just too horrible.

"Have you heard about Gloria, the lunch lady?" the little girl next to him said. "She yells all the time — that's what my sister told me."

"No," said another boy. "That's Mrs. Twig. She's hard of hearing. She can never hear what you say, and she gets the change mixed up all the time."

"What's for lunch?" Clyde said softly. There was no answer from anyone. Then a very small voice said, "I sure hope it's not soup."

"Or mystery goosh," said Clyde.

"I wish Jell-O."

Clyde decided right then to stand in line next to the girl who wished for Jell-O. Her name was Rosemary.

Clyde's class marched single file down the stairs, along with the other grades. Everybody looked bigger and more ready for lunch than Clyde would ever be.

Clyde suddenly wished he could skip lunch completely.

"I have a stomachache," he whispered. But no one heard him.

"Let's move that line!"
Clyde saw something large
and shadowy in the doorway.

It must be Gloria.

Clyde had a close-up look.

Gloria was big and lumpy. She wore a spidery hairnet and had big tufty eyebrows.

"Both hands on the tray," she said, turning toward Clyde. "Oh, you must be Jefferson's little brother. You look just like him. What's your name?"

"Clyde."

"What's that? I can't hear you," she said. Her voice was large.

"Clyde."

"What? Right here, sonny." And this time she bent over and pulled him toward her ear.

"Clyde! What a nice name. It rhymes with *slide*. And that's what you have to do — slide the tray along the counter, okay, Clyde? Slide!" She chuckled.

"Okay," Clyde said.

Clyde took his tray.

"Sweetie?" Another lunch lady behind the counter held up an ice cream scoop. "You want some?"

"It's mashed potatoes, not ice cream," whispered Rosemary to Clyde.

"Weird."

There were green beans, too, and something in a bun with catsup called Sloppy Bens. And there was Jell-O.

But it was very strange Jell-O. Stiff and carved into little cubes. It didn't shake or shimmer like the Jell-O that Clyde's mom made.

Finally they came to Mrs. Twig, the money lady. She seemed very old. Clyde was worried. Would she be able to see his money?

Rosemary gave old Mrs. Twig her money. She did it perfectly and was now heading toward a lunch table for first and second graders.

It was Clyde's turn. "I have the exact change," he said in a loud, clear voice.

"Thank you, sonny." Mrs. Twig nodded and smiled.

Now for the last hard part — to pick up his tray and carry it to the table. He could see Rosemary ahead of him. Oh, dear, he thought. There was some spilled juice on the floor, and she was heading right for it. Suddenly he saw her skid.

She hung on to the tray. Clyde felt his breath freeze. The dish of Jell-O went flying off.

The little ruby red cubes of Jell-O were spinning through the air. They bounced off the floor in *boing-boing* jumps before they finally stopped.

Oh, no! Clyde thought. Poor Rosemary! He remembered how the lunch ladies never help you clean up.

"Come on, Rosemary, I'll help you," Clyde said. Rosemary was trembling.

"Come on. It's just the Jell-O. All your other food is still on the tray."

"They're laughing at me." Rosemary sniffled.

Then a big, soft shadow slid over them.

"No, no sweetie! They're laughing at the stupid Jell-O. Who ever heard of Jell-O that *boings*?" It was Gloria. "Let me help you here." Her immense lumpy body seemed to fill up the air around them. "Awfully nice of you to help, sonny. What did you say your name was?"

"Clyde. I mean, Clyde."

A table of fourth graders started to snicker. Gloria glared. "Listen to me! There'll be no laughing, no uncalled-for remarks. We've had an accident here." The table fell silent. There wasn't a single snicker or chuckle — not a word. A little second grader climbed down from her chair and began to help.

Soon all the Jell-O cubes were picked up. Clyde and Rosemary found their way to their lunch table and sat down. "Here's some new Jell-O for you, sweetie," Gloria said. "*Boing-boing* Jell-O!" Rosemary giggled.

"You wished for Jell-O," Clyde said.

"Yes," she said quietly. "And I wished for a friend, too."

"You did?" Clyde said. "So did I." And he forgot all about his worries.

That night, Clyde helped his mother serve dinner.
"Why look at Clyde!" said his father proudly.
"Watch out for that milk!" muttered Jefferson.

But Clyde held the tray steady, and the milk did not spill —
not a single drop.